You Just Might Believe It

*Stories with fact and fiction
about real animals*

by Dorothy A. Smith

Sketches by Gabi Aicher, LauruS Myth,
Jessica Regan and Angela Smith

Copyright © 2014 by Dorothy A. Smith

You Just Might Believe It
Stories with fact and fiction about real animals
by Dorothy A. Smith

Printed in the United States of America

ISBN 9781629525112

All rights reserved solely by the author. The author guarantees all contents are original and do not infringe upon the legal rights of any other person or work. No part of this book may be reproduced in any form without the permission of the author. The views expressed in this book are not necessarily those of the publisher.

www.xulonpress.com

CONTENTS

About the Book ix
About the Author xi
About the Artists. xiii
Dedication xv
Kids Opine xvii
Acknowledgements xix
Introduction xxi

THE STORIES

Giovanna, Pino and The Doggies' Show. 25
Hugger, a Tarsier Monkey in the Philippines 43
Laurus, an Emu in Australia Myth 65
Manfred, a Blue, as in sad, Goat in Switzerland. 83

It can sense your feelings,
Your attitude, your sighs.
It can understand you,
Can read you thru its eyes.
It can communicate
With stares, snarls, a yap.
It feels rewarded
With its head upon your lap.

From "Pets" By Dorothy A. Smith

ABOUT THE BOOK
YOU JUST MIGHT BELIEVE IT

Stories with fact and fiction about real animals

There are four animal stories in this book. They are not necessarily the type of animals that you will encounter often, except for the rescued dogs. Three of the stories take place in countries across the ocean in the Philippines, in Australia, in Switzerland and one in the U.S.A.

A real earthquake in the Philippines is the setting for the rescue of a Tarsier monkey, Hugger. He is the smallest monkey in the world (three inches long), found clinging to the hand of a ten year old girl.

In Australia you'll meet Laurus, an emu. You'll become familiar with the responsibility of raising emus for profit; the bonding of animals, friendships and the beginning of the myth of Laurus.

Then in Switzerland a goat named Manfred who is not appreciated because of his harsh disposition, runs away. Something occurs that reveals his true nature and he finds value through giving freely of himself.

In the U.S.A., the land of the "Great American Dream", you'll read about a real girl, Giovanna, and her dream come true. You'll learn that dogs from a Rescue Shelter are talented, bright and lovable and most deserving of a second chance.

> The author deems the interest and reading level acceptable for ages 9 and up.

ABOUT THE AUTHOR

Dorothy A. Smith, B.S., M.A., Ed., is a retired teacher, a published poet and author. This is her third Children's book. Previously published books are: *Fragile Prisms (A Potpourri of Poetry)*, *It Never Happened (Fictional Animal Stories of Rescue)* and *The McDare Secret (A Tall Tale of a Young Boy's Journey to Gianthood)*. All are available on Amazon.

She is a mother, grandmother, great-grandmother, a Lay Carmelite, active in her community and parish, St. Joseph Church in Manteno, Illinois.

ABOUT THE ARTISTS

Hugger, The Tarsier Monkey by

Angela Smith, a high school junior doing advanced placement studies at the college level in California. She is mastering the Japanese language, perhaps to teach, and very interested in fashion design. She enjoys sketching and working with watercolor.

San Jose, California

Pino, The Italian Greyhound by

Jessica Regan, a seventh grade student. She wants to pursue a career in Graphic Design someday. She enjoys computer projects and personal involvement in art and art projects.

Manteno, Illinois

Laurus, The Emu by

LauruS Myth, a graduate of U.of CA, Santa Cruz with a BFA degree. She was presented with an Award of Excellence in the Arts along with other multiple nominations. She is a "World Art Experience Traveler" with an expanded portfolio, has studio space and creates murals to order.

San Jose, California

Manfred, The Goat by

Gabi Aicher, an eighth grade student. She loves drawing and is good at it, but really only does it just for fun. Her ambition is to go to school to study dentistry, however, she also thinks that being an art teacher would be cool.

Manteno, Illinois

Dedication

To my children, their children and their children. And to all the children who love to read for enjoyment, information and inspiration. May you be creative.

KIDS OPINE

The Emu's story was very interesting and moving. It takes you through the life of Laurus, the emu, from her birth and it is about her emu friends who are handicapped. It tells you something I did not know, that the emus are raised and used to make a profit on their body parts. I learned something new.
Jackson Baldwin
7th Grade

I believe many kids will love the story of *Manfred, the Blue, as in sad, Goat*.

Whether they read it or it is read to them they will enjoy it to the end. It should become available to people in many places such as a library, book store and even on a kindle.
Bridget Halleran
8th Grade

You Just Might Believe It

Giovanna, Pino and the Doggies' Show is an inspirational tale of a young girl following her dreams. Her love for animals and helping others is a good lesson for all. I think it is an engaging story for boys and girls at all elementary levels.

Nora Halleran
10th Grade

In the myth about *Laurus, the Australian Emu,* I appreciated the factual information about a bird, of all animals, that is very valuable for what it can provide for man. I also enjoyed the fictional part of the story, it held my attention and I recommend it to a wide range of readers.

Patrick Boarini
10th Grade

Acknowledgements

I extend my sincere gratitude

- to my family and friends who are at my beckon call, especially Annie and Jolene;

- to Erin Cunningham for her super skills at formatting and being my aide in submitting my manuscript to the publisher;

- to Giovanna Cardella for allowing me to include her dream in a story;

- to the young artists Laurel and Angela Smith, Gabi Aicher and Jessica Regan for their exceptional sketches;

- to the people who endorsed the stories, Cheryl Simanek, Therese Taylor, Gail Kikkert, Jamie Lockwood and Cassie Herman with their generous comments and recommendations;

- to the kids who read stories and submitted opinions in "Kids Opine", Jackson Baldwin, Patrick Boarini, Nora and Bridget Halleran;

- to the editors at Xulon Press for their encouraging assistance throughout the publishing process.

INTRODUCTION

The fiction in these stories is fastened together with facts that increase the credibility of the story. It's difficult to take the teacher out of this storyteller. That is why I include facts that I dig up in research of the subject.

You see, we live in a real world full of reality, but there is also the creative element in this world that inspires a writer to think, *What if...* and in this twenty first century pretty much anything goes with that thought *What if...*

In Hugger, there really was an earthquake in Bohol, Philippines. I knew the Tarsier monkey lived in the trees right there so I did a *What if* someone saved a Tarsier story. How would I arrange that?

In Manfred, goat dairies are a popular business in Switzerland so I did a *What if* the goat milk was going sour, and Manfred was to blame, and *What if* he becomes a hero. How would I arrange that?

In Laurus the Emu, I felt it was important to stress the importance of her life before she was sent to market so I did a *What if* she didn't go to market and she became more valuable than her body parts. How would I arrange that?

In Giovanna, which is part biography of Giovanna, all the dogs were rescued from the animal shelter. I did a *What if* a Greyhound, who was going to be put to sleep, does something past remarkable. How would I arrange that?

I hope you enjoy traveling through these stories and learning something you did not know. I hope you'll think of writing a creative story someday because you'll never know how far the *What if* approach will take you until you try. Soooooooooooo *What if* you try? How would you arrange that?

PINO

Giovanna, Pino and The Doggies' Show

Once upon a lifetime, there really was a young girl who started to build her dream for the future while she was still quite young. No one knew that in her head and her heart she wanted to excel at something that would make people happy. Giovanna loved to see smiling faces. If smiles were missing she said or did something that would bring back a smile. As a little girl she found that even standing on her head could make people smile, laugh and be happy.

A piece for her dream was gymnastics. As a preteen she stood out from all the other gymnasts because of her excellence. However, Giovanna did not want to be just a gymnast for the future.

You Just Might Believe It

Gymnastics gave her confidence in appearing before an audience and added success to another piece for her dream when she became a clown. She had a natural talent, but she did not want to be just a clown for the future.

Giovanna was a five foot raven haired beauty with impressive big brown eyes framed with naturally long curled up eye lashes. Her smile was infectious and sincere. Her spirit was vivacious, happy and lively, a good medicine for the people and children who needed smiles. When she developed magic trick skills her good looks contributed to the audiences' interests and attention. Again she was successful but did not want to be just a magician for the future.

One day she made a casual visit to the Animal Cruelty Shelter. There was an overwhelming amount of sadness there. It was not her intention to rescue an animal that day, but she did. She was drawn to Reginald, a black miniature poodle with a white neck and chest. He looked like he was wearing a tuxedo. The manager, Mr. x, pointed to a miniature, apricot poodle, "He is the father of this one, Lilly. I recommend they stay together," he said.

"You're right, I will take both of them," she said. "Do you have a box or a cage I can transport them in? I'd be happy to purchase a cage if you sell them."

"You may borrow the cage today and return it tomorrow. Bella's Pet Supplies on Main Street has a good selection," he replied. If the dogs don't work out my policy allows you to return them." Mr. Duggan was positive and friendly and comfortable to do business with. He valued the animals, and trusted his patrons.

Giovanna was holding both dogs and they snuggled their heads into the bend in each arm, and their pom-pom tails seemed to spin with excitement. "Reginald and Lilly," she whispered, "how lovely." "Tell me, Mr. Duggan, is there anything I should know about these two besides their being related?"

"They have had all their shots, been well cared for, the owners had the black one for four years, the little one is two, a friend took the mother. They have a life expectancy of twelve to fourteen years. The owners were moving to a "no pets" residence. You won't regret taking them," he assured her. "Just make a donation, I'll give you the paper work, and they are yours," he added as he gave the poodles a gentle petting.

Her next stop was the Pet Shop. She bought everything to make her home pet ready, bowls, food, treats, grooming needs, (including a black bow tie for Reginald, and a wide, pearl choker for Lilly), toys, beds, two cages, and a few books about poodles. She was anxious to get home and make arrangements for her new room mates.

Once they got use to their new home and owner, Giovanna discovered the poodles did tricks to entertain themselves. They walked on their hind legs, did flips and roll-overs. The amazing thing was watching them dance to "The Tennessee Waltz". Her dream was starting to take shape.

The next day, on her way to work, she returned the two cages to the shelter.

Two months later when Giovanna walked into the Animal Cruelty Shelter there was a cage on the counter. A Toy Boston Bull Terrier sat in it with his snout pressed against the grill of the cage. He was black with white here and there on his body. He had a large flat head with no wrinkles on his black forehead. His beautiful black, wide-set, round eyes were pleading for someone to cling too. "I want this dog," she said to Mr. Duggan.

"You might want to reconsider," he replied. "This dog was just dropped off, and the owner said he had too many medical problems and it was impossible to house train. I see signs of abuse. We were planning to put him to sleep even though he has a life span of fifteen years. We just can't afford him."

"Forget that!" was her quick reply. "Tell me his medical problems. I'll take him to a vet and make him better." She took out her check book and wrote a donation to the shelter. "Please, give me whatever paper work you have on him. I can't accept giving up on anyone, human or animal. I believe in the value of second chances."

"You are among the rare few, Miss," said Mr. Duggan. "Here is the paper work that the owner left with us. We have nothing to add to it. Thank you for caring, and remember our policy, you may return any animal for any reason."

"Does the cage remain with this dog? Or do you need it?" she asked.

"He came in it so he can leave in it," was his smiling reply.

After a good check-up and the necessary shots at the vet, Peanut was ready to meet the rest of the family. Reginald and Lilly were delighted and immediately started to show off their stunts. To Giovanna's surprise Peanut was quite agile and a copycat. He fell right in with the antics of Reginald and Lilly. Giovanna found there was nothing wrong with him that proper care, loving attention and patience could not cure. He was house broken in three days. Peanut was very easy going. Once his health returned, he was a real pleaser making obvious efforts to make Giovanna happy. He brought her slippers to her and the TV Guide every evening after she walked her three pets and she rested in her favorite chair. Then Peanut would cuddle closely on her lap and fall asleep.

It became more of a chore to go to work everyday because her work environment was not a joyful place and she could only spread just so much joy without being considered odd. Her smiling face and disposition was the only light in the Domestic court system. She thought about her dogs all day long. Luckily they were not barkers, which was good, and there was always music playing to keep them company. What she didn't know was that while they were relaxing they were being educated by the music. Aha! Another piece for the dream was forming.

Mr. Duggan paid Giovanna a visit early one evening. He had with him a small black and white Italian Greyhound on a leash. When she opened the door he began apologizing, "Giovanna, forgive me, but I had to come to you tonight. The inspectors will be at the shelter in about one hour. If they discover that I still have this little guy, I'll be fined and they'll have him put to sleep. No one wants him. I've had him too long, and according to the inspectors, he's too expensive to keep alive."

"Please come in, Mr. Duggan," she said with surprise written all over her face. "Do I understand that you want me to take this dog?" she asked.

"I was hoping that you would take him, Miss. You've shown a sincere concern for rescuing my dogs, and this little guy is very bright, so worth being rescued. As a toy size this is as tall as he gets, seventeen inches."

"Come with me, Mr. Duggan," she said.

He and the Italian Greyhound followed her down a hallway to the last room on the right. She opened the door to the dog room. Three walls were painted bright yellow and one was light blue. The floor was a shiny, marbleized tile. One wall was lined with dog beds with picture posters of outdoor scenes on the wall above each bed. In one corner the cages were stacked, in another corner a CD unit sat on a high shelf and soft music was playing. "This must be doggie heaven," exclaimed Mr. Duggan.

"No, Mr. Duggan, it's home sweet home," she replied. "And I think I've got room for this doggie too." She knelt down close to the dog on the leash. He was anxious to greet the yapping dogs in front of him. "I think you're handsome. Do you have a name?" she asked as she stroked his lovely black coat.

"Pino is his name," said Mr. Duggan. "Then you'll take him?" he asked.

"Of course I will. I'll come by for his paperwork tomorrow," she beamed.

"I've got everything right here in my pocket," he said hurriedly, as he pulled the papers out and handed them to her in haste. "I've got to get back to the shelter for the inspectors. I am forever grateful, Miss. I thank you. You won't be sorry, I promise you." She led Mr. Duggan to the front door. Pino remained in the dog room and got reacquainted with Reginald and Lilly. Peanut, the pleaser, brought him a bone.

A surprise awaited Giovanna when she arrived at the shelter the next day on her way home from work. Mr. Duggan introduced her to a young man who was standing at the counter. "Giovanna," he said, with a broad smile, "This is Dan Nolan. He has his own dog show. He has rescued his show dogs from our shelter for many years. Now he needs a few more." He turned to Dan and said, "Dan, this is Giovanna. She rescues dogs too."

Dan was a tall, broad shouldered, handsome man. He extended his right hand for a shake to Giovanna saying, "Pleased to me you, Giovanna. Are you in show business?"

She took his hand graciously and answered, "Same here, Dan. I've been a clown and a magician. Does that count?' she answered. The words "his own dog show" were ringing through her head.

Dan raised his eye brows and widened his eyes as he took further notice of this very attractive, almost five foot, trim, little lady in a navy, pinned striped suit with a pink blouse. She was looking up at him. "Well, of course it does. You're absolutely lovely," he said, and made her blush. "I'm looking for someone, preferably a female, to be my assistant in my "Doggies of the Wild West Variety Show." Would you be interested in an audition?"

Mr. Duggan leaned forward and said, "You may sit in the waiting room and talk in private, if you'd like."

They did. They sat across from each other. Giovanna began, "Tell me what you are looking for in an assistant, Mr. Nolan. To tell the truth, I think I'm interested, and I'm more than curious about your doggie show."

"I need someone with at least these three special traits," he began. "Number one, a love and kindness for dogs; number two, a cheerful personality; number three stamina," he explained as he held up a finger for each count. "So far you've passed on number one and two. Tell me you have confidence performing before people, and if you don't have confidence I'll teach you. I don't want to look for anyone else because I see so much potential in you," he added.

"Well thank you for the compliments," she said. "I can give you a few DVDs of me performing as a clown and a magician. I've never measured my stamina, but I think I have a good supply. Also, I really think I'm ready for a change in my life."

"I'm sold," he nodded with affirmation. "How many dogs do you have? Maybe we can incorporate them into the Variety Show."

"Right now I have four, a Boston Bull Terrier, two Poodles, and an Italian Greyhound. I've only had them for three months.

They dance and do tricks just because they are happy," she said. "How many do you have?"

"Well, I just lost two, and two more are tipping the old age scale. I have three healthy ones. I came here today to check out replacements. I'd like to meet your dogs to consider including them before I rescue any from the shelter. All my dogs are from this shelter," he explained.

"So are mine," she answered eagerly. "I really have to get home and take them for their walk. Why don't you follow me and you can meet them?"

When Giovanna and Dan walked into the doggie room, the music was playing and they received the dance routine welcome. Dan was impressed. Pino brought the dogs into calm order and that impressed Dan even more. The dogs were panting anxiously to greet Giovanna and Pino restrained them.

"Giovanna, you've got an exceptional troop here," he said. "All we need to do is write a new script to incorporate both sets of dogs, yours and mine." He was excited and enthusiastic. "Can you come to my home tonight and meet my wife, Izzy, our two daughters, Maura and Nora, and our dogs?"

"Wonderful," was her answer. "May I bring Pino?"

"Of course," said Dan. "Come at 6pm, he added, and here is my card with my address and phone number."

At dinner Izzy shared some of Dan's creativeness and that she and the girls had performed in the show, but only as helping hands. They could not make a commitment as regulars because they had many other interests. Pino was left with Dan's show dogs. They were small to standard sizes and all bigger than Pino. Giovanna's dogs were toy and miniature and friendlier. They trusted Pino. He tried to use his gifts of controlling to keep Dan's dogs calm, but they only performed on commands from Dan so Pino gave up and settled down by the dinning room door while the old doggies carried on in their own ways, chasing their tails and teasing each other.

Giovanna gave her one month notice to her boss. Two more visits to the shelter afforded her a tri color "tea cup" Chihuahua named Chi Chi. She was fragile and only six inches tall. Right next to her was a toy, seven inches tall, fluffy, white Pomeranian named Zola. Giovanna was delighted.

She had to have them because she felt others would feel the same attraction. Of course Mr. Duggan knew she would love them. Right away her mind started to flow with ideas for the dog show.

She recalled how she loved costumes as a child; how she would dress up and do her tumbling stunts; how everyone would smile, laugh and clap. *Aha, she thought,* as she drove, *I will get costumes for all my dogs. I will let them perform in their own sweet ways. People, kids will love them.* She went right to Bella's Pet Shop and bought what she thought would be a good start for costumes, and when she got home she dressed her show dogs.

Reginald, the black poodle with the white neck and chest, already had a black bow tie so she put on his new, black tuxedo jacket with white satin lapels and a pair of doggie sunglasses. "Wow! You looked so smart, so cool!" she laughed. Then she added a few things to Lilly, the apricot poodle.

She put the wide, pearl choker around her neck and clipped a beautiful pink and blue bow to her head. The long ribbons streamed down her back. Then she added a band of pearl bracelets to her front leg. "You are so beautiful, you look artificial, Lilly," she exclaimed.

"Now for you, my tiny one, Chi Chi. I'll slip you into a red tutu with a black lace top. Hold still while I get this red headband to rest on your tiny forehead. There! Your ears will keep it straight. How precious! How precious!" Chi Chi stood on her hind legs and pranced around for the doggies to admire her. "I must get her a teacup to stand in." Then she looked over at Zola, the white Pomeranian who was totally confused seeing Chi Chi all dressed up.

"Come on. Come on, Zola. I have something for you too," she said as she picked her up and ran her fingers through Zola's fluffy fur. Giovanna carefully pulled Zola's head through the neck of a red dress with white polka dots and a white lace collar. It had a gathered, full skirt and a bow that tied in the back. Her tiny polka dot hat had a strap that went under her chin to hold it on. Zola looked stunning. The dogs, though a bit confused, scampered around their room and around Giovanna while she sat on the floor and watched her very own doggie show. Now she needed to organize a show.

Giovanna called Dan and asked him to bring Izzy and his two daughters over to see what she had and to make plans for their show. By 9 o'clock that night everyone had given their thoughts, and THE NEW DOGGIE VARIETY SHOW took shape on paper.

Dan's dogs were a variety of Mutts. On Dan's commands they would continue their acts with spring-boards, trampolines and flaming hoops. Giovanna's dogs would do acrobatics, dances and comedy. Chi-Chi and Zola would look striking in their tiny costumes. Pino would act as a director wearing a top hat and tails. He had a glow wand with a sleeve on it, and he slipped his right paw into it to tap and wave it about.

Izzy suggested that Peanut and Zola do "A Bicycle Built for Two" appearance. Peanut wore a pair of knickers with suspenders and a wide, flat straw hat from the 20's. This was a great idea. Then Giovanna made her last suggestion. I could sing, dance, do acrobatics and magic tricks, and added that she could create doggie figures with balloons for all the children in the audience. By midnight all the plans were written down and everyone was filled with excitement, eager to get the show on the road.

The show drew crowds everywhere they went. This was more than a dream come true.

Besides the dancing talents of the doggies, Pino amazed people with his precise directions. One act was the finale. There was a long canvas with silhouettes of the small doggies painted in a horizontal line across the bottom. Their names were printed above each silhouette. Pino tapped his wand several times on a kettle drum and the doggies came scurrying on stage forming a circle around Pino and gazing up at him. He tapped his wand again once and they all scampered to sit in front of their own silhouette and name. Two of the doggies were not correct. Pino tapped each one with his wand, they traded places. Pino turned to the audience, waved his wand high above his head, and the audience roared and clapped with delight. He was the bright dog that Mr. Duggan said he was.

One week before the close of the County Fair in Porter, thieves broke into the show's storage van. They were in the process of loading boxes of material in the trunk of their car when Pino spotted them pushing Zola's cage into their car. The greyhound has exceptional vision. Quickly he slipped his paw into the sleeve on his director's wand, found the power control box, flipped all the lights on and also the sound system for the fair grounds. The lights blared, the music blared. Dan was alerted, security was alerted and the chase began.

Dan's special, non-performing, four foot seven inch tall, Irish wolfhound, Paddy, who was intended to guard the family and its possessions, sprung into action. He galloped after the thieves as they raced for the exit. Paddy pounced on one of the men and held him down. Pino, who had a double suspension gallop, all four feet off the ground, leaped upon the other thief and attached his teeth to the thief's black hood. The terrified thieves raised both arms in surrender to the security guards and were hauled away.

One of the tallest dogs in the world, Paddy, the Irish wolfhound, and one of the fastest, Pino, the Italian greyhound, saved the day, and saved the show.

HUGGER

Hugger, a Tarsier Monkey in the Philippines

Unexpected. Like heavy footsteps on a hollow floor, the tremors moved the earth. The earthquake came on quickly. On Tuesday, October 15, 2013, the earth started to convulse at 8:12 a.m.. It rolled and belched like a pressure cooked, then it blew its lid and the earth heaved open and started to swallow homes and trees and people. It continued to carve its path of destruction at a 7.2 magnitude scale until 3.2 million people were affected. The after shocks rumbled for three more weeks to the northern and southern extremes of Bohol province in the Philippines. When a Typhoon struck the same region in December, even more people were devastated and homeless. Pauly Santos, 12 years old and his sister, Angela, 10 years old, survived and so did a tiny Tarsier monkey which Angela named Hugger.

You Just Might Believe It

The sounds of screaming and crying were deafening. Pauly was dazed as he crawled out from under a mattress that protected him when his home crumbled like a house of sticks and slid close to the bottom of one of the Chocolate Hills that the island of Bohol is famous for. The Chocolate Hills are limestone formations that change from green to dark brown from season to season. They are a popular tourist sight. Stretching for acres, they resemble chocolate Hershey kisses during the dry season when they are brown.

Pauly felt lucky that he was not swallowed up by the wide gap in the earth that claimed many of his neighbors and their homes. The quake continued to carve open the earth in a reckless fashion as it moved both north and south through the province of Bohol. He stood there bewildered, his black air dripping wet over his deep set, large brown eyes. His tee shirt was torn as were his knee length shorts. He was barefoot and bleeding from scratches from head to toes. The branches of the trees that were uprooted as he was forced down hill with them gripped at him as he descended. The power of the earth's pitching and heaving was cruel and battering to everyone and everything in its path.

Pauly knew his parents had left earlier that morning to set up their produce stand in town, but where was his sister Angela?

He suddenly started yelling out her name in panic. With all the people through the hillside doing the same for their missing loved ones she would never be able to hear him. He dropped to his bleeding knees and began to claw away at the wet debris that cluttered the ground around him.

"Angela! Angela! An-ge-la!" he pleaded. "Angela! Angela! It's Pauly." He was frantic, digging like a dog for a bone, crying his eyes out. "Angela! Angela! Angela!"

Pauly loved his little sister and was responsible for her when their parents went to work. He had to find her. He stopped digging and began to pray his Jesus prayer, "Jesus, Jesus, Jesus, help me!" He prayed it over and over while looking up into the unusually dark sky. Warm tears streamed down his brown cheeks, and he was shaking. The earth was still rocking.

A calm, old man, who looked as battered as the rest of the people, came to his side. "Come," he said to Pauly, "I hear someone screaming under a heap of stuff over there. He pointed to the bottom of a hill. Maybe it is your loved one. Maybe it is one of mine. We can dig together."

Pauly got up off his knees, wiped his eyes on the back of his hands and followed the old man.

You Just Might Believe It

The old man spoke in Tagalog, one of the official languages of the Philippines, and beckoned to some young boys to come and help too. Together they lifted and hauled a large wooden door from the top of a heap. Then there was a couch, bottom up, which they struggled to lift away, and there was Angela, moaning. She was straddling a cushion and holding her arms close to her chest. She was protecting something and afraid to open her eyes.

"Angela," Pauly called down to her. "It's my sister," he said to the old man. "It's Angela. Help me lift her out from this mess." They immediately climbed closer to her and began to clear off the soggy stuff that was cluttered on top of her. And they discovered why she had her arms so close to her chest. They saw that a monkey, a Tarsier monkey, was hugging her wrist and thumb. It was clinging for its life and it's extremely large googly eyes looked petrified. All around her were many Tarsiers that did not survive the thrashing and up heaving of the trees they lived in. This sole one found Angela and lived. She protected it from any further danger by holding it close to her heart and breathing.

When Angela opened her dark, teary eyes and saw Pauly, she began to cry and shake. "Pauly," she cried, "You found me. You found me."

"Angela, this man helped me find you." Pauly turned to point to the old man, but he was gone, only two young boys stood close by, nodding and smiling.

"Where did the old man go?" he asked the boys.

They looked at each other and asked, "What old man?"

"The old man who spoke to you in Tagalog, and asked you to come and help me find my sister."

"You called to us to come and dig your sister out," said one of the boys.

"Yes, you were screaming that she was buried. No one was speaking in Tagalog to us. We hurried to help you. There was no old man here," said the other boy.

Pauly looked up and raised his open hands to Heaven. "Thank you, Lord," he whispered softly.

He carefully helped Angela and the Tarsier monkey to safety. He hugged her and she hugged him ever so fondly. The young boys took off running to help someone else. There was much more rescuing to do.

You Just Might Believe It

"Are you alright?" Pauly asked Angela. "Do you hurt any place?"

"I think I'm fine. I don't feel like anything hurts. But you are hurting all over. Who can help us? You need some ointment for those cuts," she urged.

"I'm fine, Angela. Don't worry about me. Thank God I found you and you are fine too," said Pauly.

"Now that you have found me I'm not worried, but I'm thirsty," she added. "I can't speak for Hugger. That's the name I've given to the Tarsier. Look he still won't let go of me." She looked down at the Tarsier monkey who gripped the wrist and thumb of her right hand. His extremely large eyes starred back, petrified. Then his head gave almost a complete circle twist and his odd ears quivered rapidly.

The Philippine Tarsier monkey is considered to be the smallest monkey in the world (measuring three inches, other species measure about six inches) and scientist say it is the oldest mammal alive. They also say it is not really a monkey, and are not even sure just what kind of primate it is. It is still here after forty five million years. They are known to inhabit several Southeast Asian islands besides Bohol in the Philippines. They live in trees. Everyone in the Philippines is familiar with the

Tarsier monkey, and Bohol is a popular tourist spot. Today was a tragic day for the Tarsiers too. Many did not survive the earthquake.

"He is frightened," said Pauly, it looks like we are his family now. We will care for him, but you know Tarsiers do not do well away from their own home. Not to worry though. He is happy to be alive. Right now, I think we have to find water, and Ma and Pa. I don't even know which way to go, Angela." He was deeply concerned.

"I feel lost too. Everything is so messed up. Which way is it to town?" she asked. "Ma and Pa are probably looking for us." Angela was always full of conversation, fears and questions.

Pauly pointed back over his shoulder. "I think we should go in that direction where most of the commotion is. We'll ask people if they have seen Ma and Pa. Most of the town people know them," assured Pauly as he took hold of Angela's left hand. They began to slowly climb over the mounds of rubble being careful not to step on anything sharp because they were barefoot.

It was still morning, but dark, stormy dark, and the light, warm falling rain felt soothing on Pauly's wounds. It washed the blood away.

Groups of people were going in different directions. They were crying and calling out the names of their loved ones and they were clinging to each other as they stumbled along almost aimlessly.

It was scary for Pauly and Angela. They ached for the people. They feared for their safety and longed for their parents. There were many cries for help coming from beneath and beyond the rubble. Everyone needed help. Pauly had a silent thought, *'Maybe the old man would return to help them.'* He held on tighter to Angela as she began to stumble and slip slid over the debris riddled, non-path that they began to wander over.

She held Hugger close to her chest. Walking was difficult. They were actually climbing over everything you could possibly find in a house that was now shattered, crushed and twisted and soaking on the ground.

Angela started to stumble often and Pauly could tell she was exhausted. She had been through an awful lot of trauma for a ten year old. "Let's sit down for a while and get some rest," he suggested. Pauly turned a crate over and they both sat on it. Hugger still clung to Angela's wrist and thumb, and she continued to hold him close to her chest. Hugger's head continued to rotate 180 degrees and his large, membranous ears were in constant motion. One would think it was the circumstances that triggered his nervous movements, but no, that is just the nature of this primate who can fit snuggly in the palm of a child's hand. Awesome!

A young woman came rushing toward Pauly. "Please!" she pleaded, "Come quickly. I can hear my baby crying, but I can't reach her. Please come! Help me!"

"Stay right here, Angela. I must help this woman. Don't move. I'll be right, right back," said Pauly. He hurried off with the woman.

Angela sat watching the stream of mourning people wander past her. She sobbed softly mixing their grief with her own. Hugger kept his head hidden and was very still, perhaps sleeping.

After quite awhile had gone by, Angela felt someone sit on the crate with her. When she turned she saw it was an old man. He had a scraggly gray beard and deep-set, sad, dark eyes surrounded with wrinkles. His head was brown and bald. Around his neck he wore a loose blue kerchief which he wiped his face and head with. He was soaking wet. His voice was soft and kindly when he asked, " Would you like some water, Child?"

Immediately, she replied, "Yes, Sir."

He reached down into the leg pocket of his tan cargo pants and pulled out a bottle of water. "Here you are," he said. He twisted the cap off and handed it to her.

"Thank you, very much, Sir," she said, and started to gulp it down.

"I'm sure your little Tarsier would like a drink too," he said. "You can pour a small amount into the palm of my hand and it will lap at it."

Angela was surprised that the old man knew she was hiding Hugger because he was hidden. "OK," she agreed, and as the old man cupped his hand, she slowly poured a small amount of water into it. Hugger lowered his small head of soft, thick, rusty colored hair and quickly emptied the old man's hand with his long tongue. He continually swiveled his head and wiggled his strange ears.

"The Tarsier moves its head like that because it does not rotate its eyeballs," whispered the old man, as Angela poured more water into his palm.

"I didn't know that," said Angela. "What else can you tell me about the Tarsier? He's not my pet. I don't own him. We found each other in the rubble, and he has not let loose of me. I call him Hugger for that reason."

"Have you heard Hugger sing yet?" he asked.

"No."

"Ha, he is scared, too scared to sing right now, but he has a high-pitched voice. Tarsiers actually like to sing. The males and females sing duets. There are several different species of Tarsiers and scientists can tell them apart by their voices," he explained. "They sound delightful."

"I would love to hear him sing," said Angela, "but you are right, he is too scared to sing. So am I."

"He will sing when his heart is ready, so will you, so will we all," said the old man. He bowed his head and sat forward resting his elbows on his knees and holding his head with both hands.

"Life has many reversals of fortune," he mumbled. "We must accept the good with the bad. Don't despair."

"We still don't know how bad the bad fortune really is, Sir. When my brother, Pauly, comes back we must find our parents," pleaded Angela. "Pauly went to help a woman find her baby. Are you looking for your family too?"

"You could say that," he replied. Even Hugger is anxious to find his family." He nodded to the monkey sadly.

"I'm sure he is, I know it can't be me. Pauly and I will find a tree with other Tarsiers living in it and we will set Hugger free," she said.

"You, my child have wisdom beyond your years. I was going to advise you to do that very thing because these tiny monkeys cannot live in captivity. Away from their natural habitat they will die. I know you want life for Hugger." Then the old man pointed out that pretty soon Hugger would need some bugs, grasshoppers, moths, beetles, whatever kind of insect she could find for him. He is already hungry.

"Perhaps because you know so much about Tarsier monkeys, Sir, you should take Hugger with you to a safe habitat. "Sir, I can tell you are as worried as I am," said Angela. It will be hard for me to keep Hugger alive. I just want to find my parents alive and ok." She started to sob. She tried to stop the tears by rubbing her eyes with the palms of her hands, but they refused to stop. Hugger starred up into her face.

"It's good to cry, Child. Tears wash our pain," said the old man. He stood up and placed his hand on Angela's soaking wet head. "I must go now," he said softly, "but I will find you again."

Angela looked up into his sad eyes. He was crying too. "I will tell Pauly you found me, Sir. Tell me your name."

"Sir, is fine," he replied, "And yes, I will gladly take Hugger with me. I know right where he will be happy again." He held out a plump stick of bamboo for Hugger to grab hold of. Hugger's weird fingers let loose of Angela's hand and the round suction tips stuck to the bamboo stick. He spun his head around and his googly eyes seemed to say "Good-bye" to Angela. She threw a kiss as the old man tucked him securely down into the thigh pocket of his tan cargo pants. The old man gave a nod to Angela and wandered away with a group of people who were carrying someone they just rescued. He took hold of the stretcher to help them.

"Thank you for the water, Sir," she called after him.

She saw him wave his kerchief above his head in reply.

She covered her face with both hands and resumed crying until Pauly sat down beside her. She felt his arm around her shoulder and heard his consoling voice. "Angela, I'm back. Don't cry. Don't cry. I found some water for you. Here have a drink." He handed her a bottle of water.

"I already have one," she said, and held it up for him to see. She began to hug him and started to talk non-stop about Hugger, the water from the old man, what the old man told her, and his name. "His name is Sir, Pauly, and he said he would find me again. He went to find his family, and he took Hugger to a safe place.

He is probably just another kind old Filipino man, thought Pauly. "How very kind of him. I'm sure he is already busy helping someone else," he said. "I have some very good news for us. Pa and Ma are safe. I asked people along the way if they knew of Marlon and Maria Santos, the produce cart people in the village. Several of them said they were being cared for after their little business crumbled into the earth. They were across the road when the earth opened and swallowed everything.

They were spared. Thank God! But, Angela, they were injured. The people could not say how badly. We must get to them. They are very worried about us."

"Let's get going, Pauly. It will soon be too dark to even see where we are walking. We must hurry," she urged.

They began their mission again.

The rain continued as a fine mist. It was tolerable because after four hours it too was a fact of life that one could not do anything about. Pauly held Angela's hand until it slipped free when she toppled into a wide, shallow hole. The size of it surprised Pauly, but this day was full of surprises. Something hit his head and he could feel himself falling.

He was sure two men grabbed hold of Angela. Pauly thought they were rescuing her, but he was wrong. Instead, they hurried away with her. She did not have a chance to scream because they quickly slapped tape over her mouth. She lashed and kicked at the men to no avail. They disappeared in the dark and Pauly stood dumb founded looking down where Angela was moments ago.

His heart began to race. When he found himself in the hole of mud and slime he could not even see a shadow of a person through the dark mist.

He dashed off in one direction screaming "An-ge-la! An-ge-la!" Then he turned and dashed in another muddy direction, then another, screaming all the time, "An-ge-la! An-ge-la!" He seemed to be in a dark tunnel. His head was swollen and sore where something hit it, and Angela was gone.

He felt sure that the men dragged Angela to what was left of a house that had only three sides and no roof. This house was forced to slide down hill and crumble as the internal quakes forced it to break loose from its simple foundation. The house landed on a narrow cliff and overlooked a forest that was unharmed by the quake. What was left of the house was unstable and could slide off the cliff at any time.

They tied Angela's wrists and ankles, plopped her down on a soaking wet floor, and left. No words were spoken.

When Angela's eyes adjusted to the dark surroundings she could make out that someone else was close by, sitting, huddled in a corner. Just a few feet away from her five other children were huddled. They had tape over their mouths and their wrists and ankles were tied with rope. They were as helpless and bewildered as Angela. Eventually, surrounded by the wet darkness and exhaustion, they gave in to falling asleep.

It seemed like hours later when Angela awoke to a high pitched musical sound coming from the trees below the cliff. Immediately she knew it was the singing of the Tarsiers that she had never heard before. It was just as the old man said, delightful. She closed her eyes and listened. *"I think they sound like many violins, soft and far away. They stop and start, stop and start. I guess they are duets, groups of duets. I wonder if Hugger is singing. I wonder if the old man is listening to the songs. I wonder if the old man will find me again. I wonnn derrr."*

"Angela! Angela! It's me, Pauly. I found you! I found you!" he cried. She was on the floor of what was left of a house, three sides and no roof. It could easily slide off of the narrow cliff.

"Pauly! Pauly!" she weakly exclaimed. "Did you take the tape off of my mouth? Did you untie my hands and feet? Did you free the other kids?"

She rattled off question after question. "Look, Pauly, this is Hugger," she continued. We rescued each other." She held up her right hand to show that a Tarsier monkey had taken hold of her wrist and thumb. "I call him Hugger because he will not let go of me. He needed to hold on to something and I was all he could find." Pauly looked but there was no Tarsier monkey on her wrist. "What day is it, Pauly?" Angela asked, and rubbed her sore head.

Pauly said, "Hold on, Angela. One question at a time. There was no tape on your mouth, your hands and feet were not tied, there are no other kids here, you do not have a Tarsier monkey anymore, and it is still Tuesday. You must have had some wild dream while you were lying there on the floor." He was calm and caring as he cleaned her off. He was thrilled that she was still alive. "Do you think you can walk?"

"I think so," she replied as she held on to his arm to stand.

"Come then. Pa and Ma are waiting for us," he said. "Hold my hand."

Together they climbed and crawled, and stumbled their way toward town.

"Oh look!" Angela exclaimed, "There is Sir." She began to call out to him.

"How do you know who he is, Angela?" Pauly asked.

"He is wearing a blue kerchief around his neck. He uses it to wipe his face and head when he gets too wet. Sir! Sir!" she called.

The old man walked slowly toward them. He did not appear to recognize them and asked, "How may I help you?"

When he got closer Pauly recognized him as the curator of the Tarsier Habitat in Bohol. His class had visited the Habitat in September. "Mr. Rectho," he said. I am Pauly Santos and this is my sister, Angela Santos. She rescued a Tarsier. She called him Hugger."

"Yes, indeed she did. God bless the two of you," said Mr. Rechto.

"I thought your name was, Sir," said Angela.

"You may call me that," he answered. "How heroic of you, Child, to rescue the Tarsier. Their lives are endangered. Hugger is now in a safe home." He spoke softly and kindly and looked into Angela's eyes.

"Now I know why you know so much about the Tarsiers," she said.

"That's my job," he answered.

"Pauly and Angela," said Mr. Rectho, "You must come to the Tarsier Habitat when things get straightened out. I would like to see you again. So would Hugger." The old man smiled kindly, turned and walked away as he whispered, "I'll find you again."

Angela heard him. "Thank you, Sir!" she called after him. "Thanks for getting Hugger to a safe place."

He waved his blue kerchief above his head in reply, and disappeared into the lamenting crowd of people.

Pauly and Angela felt a warm sense of satisfaction that comes from doing the right thing. They could hear their parents calling to them. They were just a short distance away, waving at them. Their feet took flight as they hurried to them. "We found you! We found you!" They all cried. They hugged and kissed.

It was dark, about 1:15 p.m., only five hours since the earthquake changed their lives, the lives of the Philippine people and the population of the Tarsier Monkeys. There was still much rescuing to be done, and many more tears to be shed.

LAURUS

LAURUS The Australian Emu MYTH

This story is a myth, a once upon a time story, about an Australian Emu whose origins go back some eighty million years. The emu's name is Laurus, a lovely name which denotes fame and honor, unveiled with remarkable thinking skills in this story.

The Emu is a flightless bird with wings that are no longer useful, and a body that provides countless commodities for people all over the world. On the Donaldson Ranch, where Emus are raised for profit, Laurus stands out from all the other Emus. At six feet six inches tall, she is the tallest, the brightest, and has the most personality. Most Emus are rather aloof and docile, but Laurus is curious to the point of being nosey, and friendly to the point of conversing with other Emus. She is bright enough to understand the meanings of the booming, drumming and grunting sounds that the Emus create. The sounds are expelled from a special sac in the throat and can be heard for miles. They have a strange language known not only to Emus, but to the animal kingdom. Emus comprehend each other, however, most Emus are not interested in conversation. They are the docile ones. Laurus was not one of them.

Laurus hatched from a beautiful glass-like looking, greenish black egg that measured over five inches. It was nested with twenty, or so, other egg in a skuzzy looking nest created by both parents out of a mixture of mud with leaves, grass, tree bark, and twigs. It was a large mess sitting on the ground and watched over by the adult Emus. The father sat upon the eggs for eight weeks. He did not eat or drink and lost weight protecting and keeping the eggs warm until they hatched. They are loyal to their family.

After about fifty-six days the incubation time was complete. Laurus and the other Emus started to peck their way out of their shells. They arrived at intervals of several days into the bright, welcoming world of the Donaldson Emu Ranch. The Donaldsons, six of them, Bart, the manager and the ranch hands, stood by ready and anxious to tend to their needs. Or rather, to supply the food and water that the male parent needed to nourish the newborns. He did not have to seek out food because everything was sorted in bins close by for the parent to gather from and deliver to the wide open mouths of the baby Emus. The Donaldson boys filled the bins with small fruit and berries, flowers and soft leaves, insect larva, caterpillars and seeds. Close to each nest was a low trough of water. They did not feed the birds, the father Emu parent did that for the first few weeks. The fledglings were on their own from then on. Everything they needed was provided on this Ranch that grooms Emus for market and for profit. It's a business.

The new born Emus looked like balls of black and tan yard until they started to slowly move. They had speckled heads and black strips down their neck and back. They appeared to have a somewhat cross, "leave me alone", look on their faces. Their beaks were long and sharp as were the three talons on each foot with toenails as sharp as a knife. When this group of young finally stood, they measured seven to ten inches tall with an outstretched long neck. There was definitely an oddity about this bird whose wings gave tiny flutters that looked like they were merely attending to an itch. All eyes were focused on the outstanding event of the day on the Donaldson Emu Ranch. Another crop, so to speak, had started to grow.

The Donaldson children took delight naming the Emus. This was a practice that the family allowed for several years. It taught the children the value of the Emu that has a history going back thousands of years. They gave them playful names like Grand Georgie, the Duke, Grand Charlie Boy, the prince,

Grand Dundee, as in Crocodile Dundee. Then they gave them their very own names. "This one is mine. I'll call him Jimmy Emu," announced Jimmy, the ten year old.

"I got mine picked out too, "Hi! Willy Emu," said Willy, the eight year old.

"Here is the strongest one," said Matt. "Look, he eats faster and more than the others. He's going to be bigger too." He clapped his hands twice. The Emu twitched his head to look right at Matt. "Yes, Mega Emu, you are mine," declared Matt, who was thirteen, the oldest of the children.

Mrs. Dondaldson took six year old Grace Anne by the hand and led her around the nests. Grace Anne touched each fuzzy head and said a female name that started with the letter "E". "Emma, Ethel, Eva, Emily, Essy, Elle, Edith, Effy, Etta, Essa," she read the names from a notebook. "I can't think of any more "E" names, Mom," she said, "and I'll never remember one from the other they all look alike to me."

"That's fine, Grace Anne, I think we have enough names for now, children, but I want to call this one Laurus," she said. This Emu was off to the side of the nest observing every little move that went on around the nest. Mrs. Donaldson had watched her from the moment she broke out of her egg. "She reminds me of a flower just opening, looking lovelier with each petal. Her bright blue eyes have a special twinkle in them. *There is no white in the Emu eyes, that's where all the color is revealed.* For a new born she is quite alert, and somewhat different from the others. Just look at how lively she is. Look how in charge of herself she is, with that 'I'll do it myself' attitude. The others are so shy."

The children observed the eyes of this Emu. So did Mr. Donaldson. "You are so right," he said. "And look, she is starting to stand already. The others are not even attempting to stand. She has that twinkle for a reason, Dear."

"And she seems to question every bit of food that her father puts into her mouth," added Mrs. Donaldson.

"Why do you suppose that is?" asked Willy. "The others are eating like they can't get enough. No questions asked."

"Look," said Matt, who was sure he knew better than the others, "She's just nosey, that's all. She's just another Emu." He dismissed the special attention given to Laurus because he wanted to focus on the Emu he chose, Mega Emu. For some reason Mega Emu had a peculiar nodding with his head that gave Matt concern. Eventually he would discover what it was.

Laurus was twelve inches tall, taller than most Emus at birth. She stepped out of the nest and took slow, deliberate steps toward Matt. She stopped, looked straight up into his blue eyes and looked him over like she was the chief inspector. Then she turned her fuzzy head and looked the rest of the family over, up and down, side to side, round and round. They were simply amazed with her behavior. Mega Emu could not move his head like Laurus, or the other Emus, for that matter.

"We've had this Emu ranch for fifteen years and never have I seen the likes of this Emu," declared Mr. Donaldson. "Mama, you are so right, she is different. I would even say special."

"Oh, boy! I'm in trouble," said Matt. "I bet she understands every word we're saying too, and when she's older she's going to kick my 'you know what.' Sooo sorry, Laurus." Matt crouched down close to Laurus as he spoke and looked into her unusual large eyes. She glared at him and rolled her eyes around, blinked her hairy lashes and then she gently pecked his hand.

"Wow!" he exclaimed. "I think she does understand people talk. I'll only tell her how beautiful she is from now on." He brushed his hand softly, ever so softly, over her downy soft, smooth beige and black stripped back.

"I want to touch her too," said Grace Anne. She squatted down close to Laurus and touched her unusual feathers. "They feel like my silk pillow, Mom." Laurus tilted her head this way and that as she examined Grace Anne. Then she stretched her neck and straightened up her body showing even more curiosity. In a split second she rubbed her head on Grace Anne's arm.

"I love her, Mom. I hope she never goes to the F. P. O. P." (For Profit Only Plant)

"You know the rule, Grace Anne. You boys understand the rule too. We are not to get attached to the Emus. Our job is to care for them. They are only passing through our ranch." Mrs. Donaldson spoke kindly but firmly.

The children shook their heads up and down. "We remember," said Matt. "We can observe them from a safe distance. Grace Anne, you can come with us to the loft in the barn every now and then. OK? It's fun to sit up there and watch the Emus and listen to their odd noises as they talk and communicate. "It is so weird. I'd love to know what they are talking about."

"OK!" was her quick reply.

After one year of growth, Laurus reached her full height, six feet six inches tall. Most of her fine chick feathers were shed, as were the new born stripes, and fluffy irregular length feathers replaced them. Each quill had two feathers. There was no vein in the feather so it was thin and not stiff. They just seemed to droop and hang loosely. Laurus spent a lot of time preening until her white base feathers and the top blackish brown feathers looked smooth and untangled. Her feathers were not really beautiful and not really pretty, just dull. She weighed about 110 pounds. Her long neck had shades of pale blue that showed through the sparse feathers growing there. She was a striking looking bird, somewhat elegant! Even arrogant! But not pretty.

The Donaldson Ranch spanned one hundred fifty acres with ten huge shelters, one every two acres. The shelters were provided for the Emus for when the rains came, or the winds, or the intense heat or just for a place to bed down for the night. Number Seven was a fenced enclosure because only the Emus with any type of handicap were housed there. Bart visited Number Seven daily. He had to make sure no further injuries occurred. There were Emus who could not walk because of poor development; some who never moved from a sitting position and needed to be washed down daily; some who could not see well and needed to be feed. They were not sick or diseased, just handicapped and not prime material for sale.

There was Spencer, "the Sensor", Bart's special Emu, and Spencer's close friend Sy, "the Eye" who never left Spencer's side. Spencer was born with weak legs. Bart wrapped his legs with a hemp rope so he could walk and put weight on them. He walked with a limp and could not run. Sy was born with one red eye and one pearly eye. There was no vision in the pearly eye and the red eye never closed, even to sleep. Spencer, a rather unsociable, sullen bird, had pity for Sy and though Spencer grumbled much, he allowed Sy to remain close to him, even preened his feathers often. Such kindness seemed unusual for Spencer. These two were the best of friends. Then there was Short, Sad Sadie. Her growth stopped at four feet and she was quite thin. From birth she had tears in her eyes, and never spoke. Laurus looked after her. Eventually, Short, Sad Sadie became Laurus' shadow and followed her around Shelter Seven when she visited.

Spencer had a giftedness of sensing the weather and trouble. When Bart became aware of this talent he created a line of three foot tall letters with a red lever in front of each letter. He taught Spencer how to communicate his talent by tapping the red lever to flip the appropriate letter up against the shelter wall. The letters were "R" for rain, "W" for wind, "H" for hot, "T" for trouble. It was a rare talent, for sure. It appeared Spencer could read, and no other Emu possessed his talent. Bart respected it and agreed with the forecast all the time, but when "T" went up he acted with haste and inspected the shelter. Sometimes the "T" meant he, Spencer, was very irritated about some little thing. His booming sound was quite annoying and Bart would talk quietly to him as he stuffed a handful of berries into his beak to calm him down. Sometimes the water in the rain trough was low, up went the "T". Sometimes Mega Emu was eating too much, up went the "T".

The grassland of the acreage was used for open grazing for the rest of the Emus, and Laurus wandered freely throughout the whole area everyday. She eventually visited each shelter and communicated with many of the Emus.

Number Seven shelter was her favorite place to visit. Spencer and Sy were her favorite friends and she would often encounter Matt in Number Seven visiting Mega Emu, whose neck was wrapped in hemp because of a severe weakness. Mega Emu was rotund, too fat to move about, and young Matt would take him for walks to give him exercise. Mega Emu was getting too heavy for young Matt. He would soon just visit and not demand exercise. Spencer sensed it and grunted his thoughts to Laurus. *This is not good.*

One day, Laurus arrived and found Spencer walking circles in the grass. He was disturbed and making horrible booming sounds. The letter "T" was up on the outside of the shelter. Laurus came up beside him and joined him in his circling about. "What's going on? And why is the "T" up?" she gurgled.

"Poachers," he replied, and rolled his head around in a wild, crazy fashion. "They are stealing us," he continued, and his eyes grew large and wild as his head continued to bobble. "Stealing us! Stealing us!" he boomed.

"No Spencer, they are the F.P.O. P. people."

"Poachers! Poachers! They came last night... took Number Seven Emus! Look inside! BOOM! BOOM! BOOM! "My sound was locked inside! Like Sadie's! I was flipping the T! BOOM! BOOM! BOOM! BOOM! BOOM!" He was hysterical. He couldn't stop raging.

Laurus went inside the shelter. There was much disorder. She looked around and could not find Sy or Mega Emu. Short, Sad Sadie was a mess. She was huddled in a corner in a pool of tears.

Laurus turned and rushed outside and began to trot her nine foot strides to shelter Number Ten where Bart was. She could still hear Spencer. She was dripping in sweat when she spotted Bart and got to his side immediately. Bart was startled when she poked his back repeatedly. Then she turned and broke into her nine foot stride gallop back to Number Seven. Bart knew there was something wrong and called out to his crew, "Follow me!" as he jumped into his jeep and headed after Laurus.

When he got closer he could see the "T" on the side of Number Seven. He could hear Spencer booming and acting in a manner he had not seen before. He went to Spencer and stood directly in front of him. He clamped both hands around Spencer's roll-about head and looked into his eyes to see if he had become deranged. "Stop!" he shouted repeatedly, and drew Spencer's head to his chest to comfort him. Laurus stood at the shelter door waiting patiently for Bart to break away from poor Spencer.

Inside the shelter Bart and the crew assessed the damage and counted that at least ten Emu were missing. "Poachers!" he exclaimed. "They'll be back for more. We'll be ready, boys! We'll be ready!" He looked up at Laurus who stood six inches taller than him and said, "Thank you, Laurus." She went and stood next to Spencer whose legs were wobbling. "And thank you too, Spencer." He added.

For two weeks Laurus stayed outside, a good distance from Number Seven and Short, Sad Sadie stayed beside her, crying and crying. They slept in the tall grass. Laurus still managed to be alert because she did not require long periods of sleep. Spencer had sensed more trouble and on night fourteen he tapped the button to turn the "T" up against the side of the shelter. Bart saw it as he made his rounds and alerted his crew. They took their positions and waited with their ambush plan.

At 3:30 am Spencer smelled the fuel of the poacher's truck and came outside of the shelter in a panic looking for Laurus. Together they hurried to where the poacher's truck was parked. Laurus remembered when Bart had a flat tire his jeep could not go far, so with her strong legs and extremely sharp toenails she kicked and slashed the tires on the Poacher's truck. Spencer could not assist her because of his weakened legs, but he began breathing his booming sound which brought Bart and his crew merging on the poachers who were already tying ropes around the necks of the Emus they planned to steal.

The poachers raced to their truck which could go no where. Laurus saw to that. Spencer began to make the booming sounds from his throat, so did Laurus, so did the grateful Emus who were not stolen from the shelter. It was like their Hallelujah. Bart and the crew tied the three poachers' hands behind their backs and marched them to their jeeps. They were going to deliver them to the authorities. They drove away and they could still hear the thunder of the Emus booming miles and miles away.

This excitement was too much for Spencer. One night shortly after the episode, he went to sleep and never woke up. Laurus never slept much after this event and she became more protective of Short, Sad Sadie. She still made her visits to the shelters always looking for another Emu to befriend. She took it upon herself to flip the letters on the shelter and trained Short, Sad Sadie to do it too. The signs for Rain, Wind and Hot were never accurate. The letter "T" never went up again. She could not sense Trouble like Spencer, but she could sense sickness, and would hurry to Bart in time to save the health of an Emu before others were affected. This was a rarity.

In due time, the selected healthy Emus were scheduled to be picked up from all the shelters, except Number Seven, by the F.P.O.P. trucks to leave the Donaldson Ranch. Laurus and Short, Sad Sadie hid in the tall grass with their heads down to avoid the sight of the Emus marching into the trucks. Both had tears.

The F.P.O.P. trucks took the delivery of Emus to factories where the resources from the Emus are sorted and prepared to ship to other markets in Europe, Asia, Peru and the United States.

These markets will select the feathers to be used in manufacturing furnishings, art, and clothing accessories. They will select the hides and legs to manufacture leather goods, boots, purses, and belts. The eyes, toenails and beaks will go to a crafts and jewelry market. The Emu fat is used to produce oil for cosmetics, and therapy creams. Of special importance is the meat of the Emu. It is not considered poultry but a beef product and has been marketed since 1990. It was an important source of meat for the early Australian and European settlers. Of course today we have many more meat choices, and you really won't see Emu in the meat refrigerators in our grocery stores. It is not a high demand meat in the United States.

Laurus was more valuable to the Donaldsons than her body parts. She was very special, and continued to live on the Ranch. She grew old gracefully, still looked elegant when she was thirty years old. That's pretty old for an Emu whose life expectancy is ten to twenty years. Short, Sad Sadie was Laurus' shadow to the very end.

MANFRED

Manfred
A Blue, as in sad, Old Goat
In Switzerland

Once upon a time, and only once, there was an old blue Goat named Manfred. He was a white goat, but he was blue, as in sad, very sad. Manfred was shaggy, shabby, ugly and a malcontent old goat in the Saanen Valley in Switzerland. In fact, his disposition was so glum and rebellious that it caused the Saanen goats to produce sour milk. On this dairy farm known for its excellent quality of goat milk, this was not good. Trouble was brewing.

Manfred sat idle in the grass outside the milking barn. He only raised his head to roll his angry red eyes and bleat deep, threatening sounds at the goats filing into the barn for milking. When they caught sight of him they scurried forward to get far away from him. He had become notorious for butting them with his exceptionally long horns causing injuries, and a stress level that caused their milk to curdle. The Saanen milking goats were of a gentle, friendly nature and very easy to upset. Not a good thing on milking days.

On this day, Lars, the foreman, Mr. Gordon, the owner of the farm and his son Alexander, stood outside the milking barn. Lars kept a keen eye on Manfred. Manfred looked away but held a sharp ear to the conversation that Lars was having with the other men. He was a wise old goat.

"Lars," said Mr. Gordon, "we are going to have to get Manfred prepared for sale by Friday. A rancher from the Valley of Thun, northeast of us, is coming to take him off our hands. Will you see to getting him prepared?"

"Of course, Mr. Gordon. Is this decision as a result of reading the log I kept on his behavior? Did you agree with the outcome that indicated each time he caused a disruption our goats produced curdled milk?"

"Absolutely, Lars. Alexander kept one of his observations on the range. He entered the number of injuries inflected by those grand horns too. We decided last night that he must get off the farm as soon as possible or we'll go bankrupt."

"I will see to removing the bell from his neck, said Alexander and sending him through the spray machine to clean him up. He's had that bell on since he wandered into our herd as a kid over ten years ago. It's not going to be easy taking it off," said Alexander. "Giving him a spraying is not going to be easy either. It's been years since he's been groomed."

"Great! I'll see to all the paper work for the sale," answered Lars.

When the men and the goats were all inside the barn, Manfred got up from his resting spot. He heard enough to make up his cunning mind. *I'll save them a lot of trouble. I'm out of here. If I have to go someplace else, it is going to be where I choose to go. I'm not waiting around for the send off,* he told himself, and started his slow walk north. He walked for three long days and nights. By Friday he had started to ascend Mt. Orion, fifteen miles north of his home of over ten years. He looked upward. *When I reach the top I will be closer to peace and the constellations,* he told himself. He began to feel relief and the "peaceful strength" that his name denoted was starting to flow back into him. Manfred was free.

Alexander searched the farm and grassland for him, but to no avail. If he was there he would stand out because of his height and mass of disheveled, unsightly, dirty fur. Clearly Manfred had disappeared with his bell on.

In the springtime on the dairy farm all eyes and interest turned to the birth of two kids, baby goats. They had the pure white, prime, choice color of the Saanen goat breed and were quite small. The frisky, friendly little females were named Roey and Zoey and in no time they were out grazing with the other goats. They were so taken up with playing and romping that they wandered further and further away from the herd, but were always in the round up at the close of each day until one day they went missing. It had started to snow, and it was a pleasant distraction on the dairy farm.

Winter arrived early with this downfall of snow that appeared to know no end. The kids enjoyed the beginning of the accumulation. They rolled and tumbled with happy bleats. Then they fell asleep curled up together. The snow continued through the night and into the next day. At noon the search began for the little ones. Looking for white in the white surroundings was extremely difficult. Even Barney, the herd dog, was confused.

Manfred looked down from the high precipice and his sheltered location on Mt. Orion. He observed the farm hands pulling sleds and searching toward the south. *Something urgent is going on down there,* he thought. When he saw the small lumps of snow bob up and down in the mounding snow, he knew they were young kids. He knew that was who the urgent search was for. He knew the farm hands were going in the wrong direction. *There is something I must do,* he thought. He decided to descend from his place of safety.

The sun melted a pathway down for his cloven hooves. He spread the two toes on each hoof to improve his balance and the rough pads on the bottom of each toe made his grip firm. It is more difficult climbing down. At one point he had to jump about ten feet in a single bound which he did without hesitation and landed closer to the bottom on a flat plateau. There he was able to look out over the whiteness and saw the snow bobbers. He leaped again from the plateau and landed in the snow that covered half way up his legs. Then it was a real trudge through the snow toward the lost kids. He shook his head and rang that bell around his neck to attract them. Manfred bleated to them. They bleated back and eventually rolled into him. *Now what?* he thought.

The kids took turns jumping at his bell. They enjoyed the hollow clang and the sound reverberated through the air. Manfred looked into their innocent faces and found a trusting friendship. He lied down in the snow and wedged his body back and forth then he stood up to looked at the cavity he created. Quickly he began to claw at the bottom of the body mold until the grass underneath was showing. The goats immediately got nibbling on the grass, so did Manfred.

Meanwhile the sun disappeared. The white laden sky seemed to touch the white laden earth with a blur that erased the horizon. The snow like a curtain in an open window blew around them, and the cavity filled up. Manfred got down into it, Roey and Zoey cuddled close to his warm body and made his bell clang until they fell asleep to the beating of his brave heart. *What now?* he thought.

Lars and Alexander were searching for the lost kids. They now rode snow mobiles with bright headlights. When they stopped and turned off their machines they could hear an echoing sound. It was the unmistakable sound of Manfred's bell. Then it stopped. They looked at each other, "Could it be?" asked Lars.

"I think it could," answered Alexander, "but what direction could it have come from?"

"We can't separate to search because we could lose each other in this white blindness. Let's drive slowly straight ahead. Keep your flares handy," said Lars. They did just that until they spotted the strange mound in the snow. On closer inspection with their bright headlights they could see shabby fur protruding from the mound. They looked at each other and said simultaneously, "Manfred!"

At the mention of his name Manfred stood up and the kids scrambled to their feet too. They tried to jump out of the cavity but the snow kept falling in on them. "Alexander, take the blanket and wrap it around one of them. I'll do the same for the other one," directed Lars.

"OK, but what about Manfred?" asked Alexander. "There is no room for him in the snowmobile."

"He stays," said Lars. "It was his choice to run off, and I don't think he was ever happy on the dairy farm. Mr. Gordon knows Manfred was unhappy."

"What about the sale?" asked Alexander.

"Mr. Gordon will surely understand when we explain," he answered.

"Oh, I'm sure he will understand. Once he discovered, years ago, that Manfred was a mountain goat he was sure he did not belong on a dairy farm. He has always felt that Manfred knew he did not belong and that's what made him a sad, a blue old goat," explained Lars. "I never thought his disposition would almost destroy the family business though," he added.

The two men stood there looking intently at Manfred with new emotions. Their hard feelings were gone and they had a sense of wonder about the old goat. "He obviously saved the lives of Roey and Zoey," said Alexander. That's a real turnabout in his behavior."

"Praise worthy, I'd say," answered Lars.

They got busy strapping the kids into their snowmobiles, and when they turned to address Manfred with kindly words he was gone. His tracks were barely visible in the snow. Again Manfred disappeared wearing his bell.

www.ingramcontent.com/pod-product-compliance
Ingram Content Group UK Ltd.
Pitfield, Milton Keynes, MK11 3LW, UK
UKHW041955230426
12048UKWH00008B/349